SANTA'S WISH

BY SAMUEL LANGLEY-SWAIN

ILLUSTRATED BY ANASTASIJA PUDANE

For R,K&L, my family & friends: Love always.
For everyone that needs a little Christmas.

ISBN: 978-1-9997628-0-3
Printed in the UK

First published in August 2017 - www.langley-swain.com

It's the night before Christmas, and all through the house
it's warm, cosy, quiet, we're cuddled up on the couch.

We've sent letters to Santa, school's finished, shopping's done.
It's time for a story, **MY FAVOURITE** Christmas one!

"NOW DASHER! NOW DANCER!" Dad says with a smile,

in his best Santa voice, making us laugh all the while.

"A BELLY LIKE JELLY", that's our favourite part,
of this Christmas Eve story that's close to our heart.

We finish our story, excited for the big day.
It's almost time for bed, to dream of Santa in his sleigh.

So we hang up our stockings,

set out the mince pies,

"DON'T FORGET RUDOLPH'S CARROT!"

my little brother cries.

"HAPPY CHRISTMAS TO ALL,
AND TO ALL A GOOD NIGHT"

Dad repeats from our story,

as he turns out the light.

I'm nearly asleep...
"DO YOU HEAR WHAT I HEAR?
Sounds just like jingle bells.
It sounds very near!"

We jump out of bed to search out the noise,
even though it's past bedtime for little girls and boys...

And pressed against the window is a **GIANT RED TUMMY,**
with a bushy white beard, it's **SANTA!** He looks funny!

We prise open our window.
He bounces in with a **BUMP!**

"I'd **NORMALLY** use the chimney,
but I'm getting **RATHER PLUMP**"

"What are you doing here Santa? I mean 'Old St Nick'?"
"I received your **SPECIAL LETTER**, so we're going on a trip!"

He grabs the mince pie, pops the carrot in his pocket

Then we run to the sleigh and WE'RE OFF LIKE A ROCKET!

We soar over the town, through snowflakes and stars,
ZOOMING ever so fast, we must be going far!

We reach the North Pole. The snow goes on forever.
POLAR BEARS, PENGUINS AND ELVES play together!
We finally land and wow, what's up ahead?
A glittering grotto made from **ICED GINGERBREAD!**

Santa takes us inside. There are **THOUSANDS** of toys being packed up by elves, for all the good girls and boys.

He shows us his huge pile of Christmas post saying **"YOUR LETTER, I WILL REMEMBER THE MOST."**

"Why is that?" we ask, feeling a little unsure.

"NOBODY'S EVER ASKED ME WHAT I WANTED BEFORE!"

"So, in all my years delivering everyone's gifts,
you've asked what I'd wish for. **MY WISH IS THIS...**"

"SPREAD JOY TO THE WORLD,
JUST FOR ONE SPECIAL NIGHT,
SO THAT THOSE IN THE COLD
CAN FEEL WARMTH IN THE LIGHT."

"I'D LIKE THOSE WHO ARE HUNGRY
TO HAVE BELLIES MADE FULL
AND FOR THOSE SCARED AND LONELY
TO FEEL LOVE, THAT IS ALL."

We wake up with a jolt. Was it all just a dream?
Or was Santa's grotto where we **REALLY** had been?

We bolt down the stairs, to find under the tree,
the **BIGGEST** pile of presents that you ever did see!

WOW! THANK YOU, SANTA, there's loads to go around!
In fact, we've got enough for **EVERYONE** in town!
We remember Santa's words and decide that we'll share
our Christmas with those who need extra love and care.

It's the best Christmas ever, what a difference we've made,
to the people around us, on this special day!

So from this Christmas on, we will grant Santa's wish.
WE WILL ALWAYS GIVE LOVE, THE MOST MAGICAL GIFT.

THE END